MOONLIGHT
Magic

StripeS

CONTENTS

I DON'T LIKE THE DARK

Anna Wilson

The sun was setting in the clear blue sky. It was going to be a cold and frosty night. Deep in the forest, all sorts of animals were waking up, stretching and yawning – then chattering excitedly as they remembered what a special night it was. It was Christmas Gathering Night! Everyone would soon be busy collecting food and finding beautiful pine cones, brown leaves, twigs and berries with which they would decorate their homes.

In her neat little house in the hollow of a tree, Ma Hare was getting as excited as everyone else. She was *so* excited that she had not noticed her son, Small, looking rather upset.

"Come on, Small, dear," Ma said, reaching for Small's paw. "Time to go Christmas Gathering."

"No," said Small. He bounded out of Ma's reach.

Ma Hare frowned and jumped over to him. She pulled his ear gently. "You can't stay here on your own," she said.

"I am *not* coming outside. It's too cold. And dark." Small shivered.

"Nonsense," said Ma. "You're a big boy now. All hares need to learn to forage at night. It's time you did, too."

"No," said Small.

Ma sighed. "All right. I'll have to find

someone to look after you, though."

Small pulled a face. "I am *not* a baby."

Ma put her head on one side. "No, of course you're not. But I'm sure your good friend Owl would like to come and see you. How about that?"

Small smiled. "All right," he said.

Ma Hare kissed him on the nose.

"Good little Small," she said. "I'll send Owl right over. And I'll be back before you know it – with all *kinds* of yummy surprises." Then she lolloped to the opening of their cosy little home and, with a flick of her tail, she was gone.

Small hopped up to the doorway. "Don't be long!" he called into the black night air.

10

The only answer was his own voice echoing back at him: *Long-ong-ong!*

Small Hare sat up and blinked.

"I don't like the dark," he said to himself.

The dark stared back at him.

"I don't think it likes me much, either," Small added.

He went back inside to hunker down in his snuggly bed and try to think warm, snuffly thoughts. But all he could think, over and over, was, "I don't like the dark."

"WHOOOOO!" A spooky noise made him jump.

"Eeek!" said Small, and he rolled himself into the smallest Small-Hare-ball that he could manage. He pulled his ears down and flattened them with his paws and tried to go to sleep.

"Whooooo!" came the noise again.

A cold breeze rushed into the tree hollow accompanied by a fluttering sound. A shadowy shape appeared in the doorway.

Small leaped up and held his forepaws in front of him, ready to box.

"No need for that," said a low, quiet voice. "It's only me – Owl."

"H-h-h-ow do I know it's you?" Small said. "All I can see is a s-s-scary shape in the d-d-dark night. I don't like it!"

The tawny owl gave an impatient, "Tu-whit tu-whoo!"

"Oh," said Small, peering out. "It is you." No one else in the wood said "tu-whit tu-whoo" except Owl.

"Of course it's me. There is no reason for you to be afraid of the dark," Owl went on.

"In fact, if you come outside with me, you'll see that it's not as dark as you think."

Small twitched his nose. "I don't want to," he said.

"Come on," said Owl. "Trust me." He spread wide his wings and ushered the shivering, shaking Small into the night.

Once out of the safety of the hollow, Small made himself look around. There were long, black shadows everywhere and spooky shapes between the trees.

"It *is* as dark as I thought," he said. "And it's scary."

Owl hugged Small tightly under his soft wing. "There's nothing to be afraid of," he said. "In fact, there are lots of animals who prefer the night to the day. Would you like to meet some of them?"

"I don't know." Small wasn't sure he believed Owl. It was far too quiet for anyone else to be up and about. But then, everyone in the wood thought that Owl was the cleverest creature of all, so maybe he should trust him...

"Urgh!" Small jumped as something flickered past him, brushing against his face. "What was that?" Small saw that there was a pinprick of light flying around in front of him.

"It's only me – Firefly," said a tiny voice.

Small realized the voice was coming from the same place as the light. "You look like a teeny dancing sun," he breathed.

"She's beautiful, isn't she?" said Owl. "You wouldn't be able to see Firefly in the day. Besides, she sleeps in the daytime."

"Sleeps?" Small sniggered. "In the daytime? What a lazybones."

"Not at all!" squeaked Firefly. "I work very hard all night, just like your ma, while *you* are being a lazybones," she teased. "I get to see all the beautiful things you miss while you are snoozing. Look at those stars!" she said, pointing her light upwards.

Small craned his neck. The sky, which had earlier looked as dark as a blackberry, was now studded with millions upon

15

millions of glittering stars. Suddenly one of them zoomed across the blackness.

"A shooting star!" said Firefly.

"Wow! Where did all those stars come from?" It made Small's head spin. He stretched his neck to see even more stars … and tumbled backwards into a somersault.

Firefly let out a tinkling laugh. "They've always been there. It's just that you couldn't see them before – it takes your eyes a while to get used to the dark," she said.

"But the stars mean it's not really dark at all!" Small said, bouncing back up on to his hind legs.

Firefly flew and twinkled around his head. "That's right."

"So, nothing to be afraid of, then?" said Owl.

Small looked ahead where the trees grew thick and close together. "It's still dark down here, though," he said in a low voice. "I don't like it. How do I know what's out there?"

As if in answer, there was a sudden scurrying and hurrying from beyond a tree trunk.

Small squealed and hid behind Owl as lots of dark shapes came rushing towards him.

"Don't be afraid, these are my friends," said Owl. "They've all been Christmas Gathering, like your ma."

Small took shelter under Owl's wing and Firefly came and sat on Small's shoulder. She cast her light over the ground in front of them and it revealed a badger, a mouse, a mole and a bat.

The creatures began chattering all at once.

"We've been foraging!"

"Would you like some of these berries?"

"Have you seen the shooting stars tonight? So magical!"

"Let's roast these chestnuts!"

Small couldn't believe his eyes. So many animals, all awake in the middle of the night.

"What have you found, little one?" asked Badger.

Small couldn't speak. He looked at Owl, who chuckled and then spoke for him.

"Small here has never been out in the dark before," he said. "And he's a little bit worried."

Badger smiled. "No need for that," he said. "Come with us and we'll show you that the dark can be your friend."

Badger held out his paw.

"Go on," said Owl, when Small hesitated. "Go with Badger. I'll be right above you."

Small took a deep breath and let Badger lead him away from the light into the trees.

"Lift your nose to the fresh night air," Badger told him.

Small did as he was told and immediately he caught a waft of the most delicious aromas. "Mmm! Buds and berries and bark!" he said. "Where are they?" He looked around wildly.

"Listen to your nose," said Badger.

Small giggled. "How can I do that?"

So Badger showed him, while the other animals followed behind, whispering and gossiping while they sniffed and foraged, too. Small found that the deeper they went into the forest, the easier it was to concentrate on the wonderful smells. Soon he had snuffled out some delicious treats of his own: berries and hazelnuts, seeds and sweet plant roots.

The animals came together in a clearing where the moonlight shone and sparkled on the stones and grass and twigs below. They heaped their treasures into a pile and sat back with a satisfied smile. There was a mound of yummy food before them and lots of pretty pebbles, pine cones and stones to use for decorations, too.

"Time for a feast," said Mouse.

"We need a fire!" said Mole.

"I'll gather some firewood," said Bat.

"I'll help," said Owl.

Badger and Small collected some stones and made a little fireplace, then the other animals helped stack firewood on top. Badger showed Small how to rub two sticks together to make a spark of fire and soon there was a warm glow coming from the firewood. The animals waited until the flames had died down and then Mouse and Mole scurried to and fro, putting nuts in among the embers and roasting berries on long twigs. Before long there was a meal for everyone to enjoy.

Warmed by the fire and the tasty food, Small felt his eyes grow heavy. His head lolled forwards and he began to tip over sideways. He woke with a start, his ears flicking back and his paws jerking up.

The other animals giggled.

"Someone's ready for bed," said Badger.

"Come on, little one," said Owl. "Hop on to my back. It's no wonder you're tired after so much excitement. I should think Ma will be home by now, so I will take you back."

The tiny hare smiled sleepily. He snuggled into the beautifully soft feathers as Owl took off and swooped low over the other animals. "Goodnight, Small! Goodnight, Owl!" they called.

"Goodnight!" Small shouted. "And thank you!"

Owl and Small returned to find Ma was indeed already back from her Christmas Gathering expedition. She ran to the doorway as soon as she heard Owl hooting hello, and opened her arms to give Small a hug.

"I hope Owl has looked after you," she said. "Has the dark been very frightening?"

"Frightening? The dark?" said Small, puffing out his chest. "Whatever is there to be frightened of? The dark is fun!"

Ma laughed. "Is that so?"

Owl nodded. "Small has grown up a lot tonight. I think he's big enough to come out foraging with you now. See you soooon!" he hooted as he flew off.

Small stood up on his hind legs to wave goodbye. "Owl's right. I *am* big enough," he said to Ma. "Look." He boxed the air with his forepaws. Then he lost his balance and fell over.

"Funny little Small." Ma Hare smiled. "Come on, let's go inside. I want you to snuggle down and be good. You've been up all night, and it will soon be morning. It's time for us to rest."

"All right, Ma," said Small. He scampered after her into the warmth of their nest in the tree hollow. He yawned and stretched and then settled down next to her, cuddling up to her warm furry body. "Can I go out in the dark with you tomorrow night, Ma?"

"Of course you can, little Small," said Ma. "We can look at the stars together. But look!" she cried, pointing at the open doorway. "It's snowing! Just in time for Christmas. Oh, Small. Isn't that lovely?"

But there was no answer: little Small was already fast asleep.

THE REINDEER
IN THE
GARDEN

Holly Webb

"Come on, Alfie!" Lucy put her hands on her hips and sighed. "Hurry up! We're going to buy Mum's present."

"I'm coming," Alfie murmured, still gazing at the reindeer. He'd thought for a moment that one of them had looked at him, with a dark, gentle eye. "It isn't long now," he whispered, "only two more days till Christmas." Then he ran towards his sister and Dad, his wellies slipping a little in the snow.

"Were you talking to those reindeer again?" Lucy demanded.

"I was only looking at them." Alfie shrugged. Lucy was always teasing him. Just because she was two years older than he was, she thought she was right about everything.

"I don't know why you have to do that every time we go past them," Lucy said. "They're just some fairy lights and a bit of wire!"

Alfie felt himself flinch a little. He didn't want to hear Lucy say things like that. Of course he knew that the reindeer were decorations. But ever since their next-door neighbour, Pete, had put them out in his front garden two weeks ago, Alfie had loved to look at them. He could just see their glow through the curtains covering his bedroom window at night, sending him to sleep thinking Christmassy thoughts. Whenever he walked by, he leaned over the wall to admire them. Even though they were made of lights, he was sure they were friendly.

"You really like them, don't you?" Dad asked him as they hurried down the road to the bus stop. "Maybe we should get some light-up reindeer next year. They'd look good next to the front path."

Alfie stopped, pulling on Dad's hand and making him stop, too. "No!"

"Why not?" Dad looked confused.

Alfie stared back at him, wondering how to make Dad understand. "Because – because they're special…" he whispered at last. He didn't want to think that the reindeer were something that anyone could buy in a shop.

Dad wrinkled his nose. "OK. Maybe just some fairy lights for the trees outside, then." He put his arm round Alfie's shoulders. "Come on, we'd better speed up if we're going to get that bus."

On Christmas Eve, Alfie was curled up in bed. Mum was baking another batch of mince pies, fresh for tomorrow, and the smell

was wafting up the stairs. Everything was ready for Christmas – the weather forecast even said that the snow was going to stay. He and Lucy had wrapped their presents for everyone – his were a bit crumpled and messy, but Alfie didn't think it really mattered. They'd left some mince pies on a plate by the front door for Father Christmas. Their house didn't have a chimney, but Dad had said it definitely didn't matter. They'd put carrots on the doorstep, too, and when Lucy had gone back in, Alfie had run over to the garden wall and gently tossed a carrot to Pete's reindeer. Just in case.

Alfie sat up on his elbows and checked that his stocking was still hanging from the end of his bed. He could just see the red-and-white knitted stripes in the light coming through the window. He rolled over and peered out between the curtains to see the reindeer. "Goodnight!" he whispered. "Hope you enjoy the carrot!" Then he pulled his duvet up tight round his shoulders, and snuggled down to sleep.

When he woke up, it took Alfie a little while to work out what had changed. He blinked sleepily at his bedroom for a few seconds – and then he saw. The light had gone – the reindeer weren't shining through his curtains any more. Properly awake now, he kneeled up to look out of the window. Perhaps Pete had switched them off? But he was sure that Pete had told Dad they were solar-powered, so he didn't bother turning them off.

Alfie dragged the curtains open.

He could just see Pete's garden by the light of the streetlamp further down the road. He squinted, trying to see the shadowy shapes of the two reindeer. It was tricky in the dark, even though he knew they had to be there.

They *did* have to be there, didn't they? It wasn't as if they could move... Alfie pressed his nose against the glass, but it only misted up with his breath. He still couldn't see them. Alfie slipped out of bed, put on his dressing gown and slippers, and crept out of his bedroom. He stood hesitating on the landing, looking over the banister and down the stairs. Where had the reindeer gone? Maybe someone had stolen them?

Or maybe … maybe something more exciting had happened. He could hear Mum and Dad watching TV downstairs – it wasn't going to be easy to sneak past them and out of the front door.

"What are you doing?" someone whispered in his ear, and Alfie jumped with a squeak.

"Ssshhh!" Lucy hissed. "You'll get into trouble."

"So will you!"

"Why are you out of bed, anyway?"

Alfie eyed his big sister doubtfully. He wasn't sure he wanted to tell her, but she clearly wasn't going to leave him alone. "The reindeer have gone."

Lucy rolled her eyes. "No, they haven't."

"They have! Go and see, if you don't

believe me! Look out of your window."

Lucy glared at him for a moment, then she darted back into her room. She came back out a few seconds later, pulling on her own dressing gown. "All right. So they have. Are you going to tell Mum and Dad? Maybe someone stole them." She looked excited. "Perhaps we should call the police."

Alfie shook his head. "No. I'm going outside – I want to see."

"See what? And you can't go out – you'll get into trouble."

But Alfie was sick of arguing. He was already gone, tiptoeing down the stairs and across the hall. He heard Lucy gasp and then her footsteps padding after him. Alfie sped up, scurrying towards the front door and twisting the latch. Then he shivered, looking out into the winter night. All of a sudden he didn't mind that Lucy was coming with him – it was very dark out there.

"I've got the key!" Lucy hissed, pulling the door shut behind her and dropping the key into her dressing-gown pocket. Alfie hadn't even thought of that. His head was too full of questions to worry about doors.

They padded down the snowy path in their slippers and leaned over Pete's wall. Now that Alfie's eyes were getting used to the darkness, he could see that the reindeer were most definitely gone.

"Someone *has* taken them," Lucy said. "That's so mean. Poor Pete."

"Poor Pete," Alfie murmured, pushing open Pete's front gate. He heard Lucy gasp behind him, but she followed him over the grass, moaning about her slippers getting wet. Then she grabbed his sleeve.

"What?"

"You'd better not go any closer – what if there are footprints in the snow? The police won't want us treading on top of them, will they?"

"I suppose…" Alfie murmured. He crouched down, peering at the space where the reindeer had been – just next to the holly tree in the middle of the square of grass. The holly tree was a fat white mound, now, and next to it was a patch of churned-up snow.

But there were no footprints. Not human ones, anyway. Just lots and lots of strange marks, almost heart-shaped, tracking across the snow. Hoofprints. There were deep lines pressed down into the snow, too, and Alfie frowned at them, wondering what they could be.

"I can't see any footprints at all," Lucy said disappointedly. "Nothing the police could use anyway."

"Can't you see these?" he asked her, pointing to the hoofprints.

"I know, but that's an animal. A fox, or something."

"Foxes have paws! Don't you see – they're reindeer prints!" Alfie gasped. "And those are sleigh tracks, Lucy, look!" He pointed to the deep lines, bouncing from foot to foot in excitement.

"Don't be silly," Lucy said. But then she crouched down to peer at them, too. "Is that what reindeer prints look like, then?"

"Yes! Lucy – the reindeer that used to be here, the light-up ones, they didn't have proper reindeer hooves. Just pointy little feet."

His sister stared back at him, her eyes widening.

"Alfie! Lucy! What on earth are you doing out here?" Dad was hurrying down the path, looking horrified. "You'll freeze! You haven't even got boots on! And you were supposed to be in bed hours ago!"

"Um – Pete's reindeer have gone, Dad…" Lucy began. "We thought maybe someone had taken them." But then she looked at Alfie and turned to gaze up into the dark, star-filled sky.

"Maybe they'll be back tomorrow," Alfie whispered.

Very early next morning when Alfie woke up, he gave his stocking a glance, just to see if it was full, then pulled open his curtains to look out at Pete's garden. The streetlights gave the snow an orangey glow, just enough for him to see by.

The prints were still there and for a moment he thought that the reindeer had

gone for ever. But then he saw them –
curled up together under the snowy holly
tree. Two dark shapes, fast asleep.

Alfie flung himself out of bed, pulled on
his dressing gown and darted into Lucy's
room. He hauled the duvet off her bed – it
was the only way to wake her up.

"What is it?" Lucy muttered, wriggling
in the sudden cold.

"The reindeer! You have to come and
see!" But she only buried her head under
her pillow. "Hurry up, Lucy, it's nearly
morning. Everyone will be up soon, and
they'll be gone." Alfie sighed, and turned to
go – but then Lucy's bed creaked, and when
he looked back she was peering hopefully
at the lumpy shape propped at the end of
her bed.

"It's so early," she whispered. "I haven't even looked at my stocking."

"Please come on!" He grabbed her hand, pulling her out on to the landing and down the stairs.

Alfie hopped around frantically by the front door, trying to get his wellingtons on as fast as he could. He wasn't sure how long it was until sunrise, and he had a feeling that once the sun was up, the reindeer would be just decorations again.

"What did you see?" Lucy whispered to him as she opened the door.

"Reindeer," he murmured back. "Real ones. I'm almost sure…"

He tiptoed out into the garden as well as he could in wellies, with Lucy following. It was still half dark and the eerie glow from the streetlights deepened all the shadows, and made their familiar road look strange. As they crept up Pete's garden path, there was a scuffling noise and the patch of darkness under the holly tree shifted. The dozing reindeer looked round at the children and one of them scrambled to its feet.

"Sorry," Alfie whispered. "I bet you're tired. We didn't mean to wake you up."

The standing reindeer stepped towards them, lowering its head, and for a moment Alfie wondered if they should worry about the huge, branching antlers. But all it did was stare at him, and then, very gently, it dabbed its soft, whiskery muzzle against his cheek. He turned to look delightedly at Lucy, and she reached out one wobbly hand and ran it down the reindeer's neck.

Alfie closed his eyes, hearing the soft huff of the great creature's breath. It nuzzled at him again, and he threw his arms round its neck in a hug.

Then he stepped back, still with the feeling of warm fur pressed against his skin, and opened his eyes. The reindeer were gone – and in their place were Pete's Christmas decorations, curled sleeping by the tree in a mass of sparkling lights.

THE NIGHT
FLIGHT HOME

Michael Broad

On a bright winter morning, Jet the jet–
black kitten woke before his siblings and
pounced on his mother. Today was the day
the kittens could go to their new homes and
Jet was beyond excited.

"When are the people coming, Mum?"
he asked, nudging her awake.

"My human family will show them in at
different times throughout the day," yawned
Mum, snuggling with her litter. "If all four
of you get chosen, we'll need time to say our
goodbyes."

"I hope I get chosen," said Jet, hopping

around excitedly. He would miss his mum and siblings, of course, but the energetic kitten couldn't wait to meet his new human family and begin a big adventure.

Just then the doorbell rang. Jet leaped on to the dining table and up to the window ledge, where he peered out into the snowy street. He couldn't see who was at the door, but moments later a girl and her mother entered the room and gazed into the cardboard box lined with blankets, where his mother and siblings still lay. The visitors were so delighted by the three kittens, all stretching and yawning, they didn't even notice Jet.

"Up here!" he mewed loudly. "Pick me! Pick me!"

The girl looked up when she heard

the racket and Jet saw an opportunity to show off his talents. The fearless kitten leaped from the window ledge to the crystal chandelier and held on tight, swinging and bouncing with the jangling jewels.

But instead of being impressed, the girl clung to her mother.

"I think you may have frightened her," said Snowflake, Jet's gentle white-coloured sister. "I'll go and see if she's all right." The white kitten crept up to the visitors and made the softest "meep". The girl smiled and picked up Snowflake, and after some gentle play she took the kitten home.

In the afternoon an elderly man arrived

and Jet showed off his balancing skills. He climbed up the curtains, walked along the curtain pole, then hopped down the bookshelves one by one. The old man wobbled as he watched the daring display and then he sat down.

"I think you've made him dizzy," said Mist, Jet's caring grey-coloured brother. "Maybe I can help calm him." The grey kitten approached carefully and rubbed his head against the old man's legs, purring loudly. The man picked up Mist and stroked his grey fur, which seemed to relax him. Mist enjoyed it, too, and was happy to be taken home.

The evening visitor was a quiet lady who worked at the local library. She sat next to the box and read her book.

Jet didn't want to risk jumping or climbing to get her attention, so he sang instead. Jet's voice was not very tuneful, but it was awfully loud. He startled the lady so much that she dropped her book.

"I don't think she can read *and* enjoy your song," said Amber, Jet's quiet ginger-coloured sister. "She might be shy – I'll keep her company." The ginger kitten curled up in the lady's lap and when the librarian finished her chapter, Amber left with her.

"I'm the only one left," Jet sighed.

As night fell it seemed there would be no more visitors. "Maybe humans don't want a kitten who likes to jump and balance and sing."

"There's a perfect human for every little

kitten," said his mother.

Jet was about to fall asleep when the
doorbell rang. The kitten sprang up
excitedly to see who had come and then
stopped in his tracks when a tall dark figure
appeared in the doorway. It was an old lady
in a long black dress with a matching cape
and battered boots.

Jet was unsure of the visitor, but the old lady brightened as soon as she saw him. She scooped him up and measured his tail, she tickled his paws and sniffed his head. When her unusual examination was complete, the old lady held him close and twirled with joy.

"How does she know I'm the right kitten?" said Jet as the lady kneeled and stroked his mother. "She hasn't seen any of my tricks. How will I know she's my perfect human?"

"When you find your perfect human, you'll know that's where you belong," said Mum. She nodded to the old lady and the old lady nodded back, and something unspoken passed between them. "I think you'll have a *magical* time together."

Jet felt very tired after such a long day

of jumping and climbing, not to mention the singing and all of the excitement, so when the old lady wrapped him in her cape, Jet fell fast asleep.

When Jet woke up the following day, he was in a willow basket beside a roaring fire in a cosy cottage. The old lady was nowhere to be seen so he set about exploring his new home.

The first unusual thing he noticed was the mice. There were black mice dashing around, busying themselves with various tasks. They sewed and swept and fetched and carried, quite unlike the mice he'd seen in his old home! Jet didn't feel any desire to chase them, and when they saw him watching, they simply waved merrily and continued with their work.

"That's very odd," said Jet.

Then the kitten heard a fluttering and flapping sound coming from upstairs, so he crept up the winding staircase and found the old woman's bedroom. She was nowhere to be seen, but there were several blackbirds flying around the room. Some were opening the curtains and others were making the bed! They saw the kitten and chirped a friendly greeting.

"Even stranger," said Jet.

Jet sat in the doorway and watched. When the birds were finished, they flew out of the open window. The kitten leaped on to the bed and then hopped on to the window ledge to see where they went.

A voice called out to him from the snowy garden below. "You're just in time for the village rounds!"

Jet looked down and saw the old woman perched on a black bicycle, looking up at him. She still wore her long black dress with the matching cape and battered boots, but now she was also wearing a pointy black hat!

She's a witch, thought Jet.

"Are you coming or not?" she asked cheerfully.

The old lady grinned up at the window

and tapped the handlebars. No one had ever encouraged Jet to make such a daring leap before, and he'd never jumped so far from so high. But the witch seemed to think he could, so he took a deep breath and leaped from the ledge. He landed on the front of her bicycle.

"Hold on tight!" she said as she pedalled away at speed.

Jet really did have to hold on tight as they zoomed down the snowy hill. He had never balanced while moving fast before, but with the witch's encouragement he soon got the knack of it.

"Lean in on the turns," she called, as they skidded across an icy puddle and turned the corner to a little cottage. The witch was there to clear her snowy garden path and when they arrived, she rolled up her sleeves and whirled her arms about.

"No broomstick?" called Mrs Bartholomew from her porch.

"Not today," said the witch as the snow swirled up in swift magical flurries and formed piles on either side of the path.

Mrs Bartholomew brought out hot chocolate for the witch and a treat for Jet, and when they were finished the witch tapped her shoulder and Jet hopped up.

"Grip with your claws when the ride gets bumpy," said the witch as the bicycle rattled along the cobbled path with the kitten perched on her shoulder. "Next stop is the village pond. The children have been hoping it will freeze for ice skating, so I think it's time we helped it along!"

"No broomstick?" called the children,

crowding round to pet Jet.

"Not today," said the witch as she kneeled next to the pond. She swirled her hand in the water and spoke a spell that crackled and crunched and turned the surface to sparkling ice.

The children cheered and took off across the frozen pond on their skates. The witch tapped her hat for Jet to jump up.

Jet now felt very confident jumping high and holding his balance, even when they skidded and bumped around, and the witch smiled with pride at her talented little kitten.

"Our last stop is Mr Major," said the witch as she pedalled up the hill. "But I'm not sure how to fix his problem without my broomstick to get up there."

Mr Major's house was cold because

pigeons had taken shelter in his chimney and he couldn't light the fire until they left. The witch was standing by the fireplace trying to think of a good spell to shoo them away when Jet had an idea.

The little kitten simply stepped into the grate and sang a song at the top of his voice, and it wasn't long at all before the pigeons took flight! Mr Major and the witch celebrated with a pot of tea beside the fire, and a saucer of milk for Jet.

After supper that evening as they sat by their own fire, Jet couldn't help wondering why the witch had not taken her broomstick out that day.

"The broomstick," said the witch, looking

up from her book.

Jet sat up straight. How had she known what he was thinking?

The witch smiled and fetched her broom from the corner of the room.

"You did so well with your training on the bicycle today, I think you're ready for your first night flight," she said, and dropped the broom in front of her. But instead of clattering on the wooden floor, it hovered in mid-air. The witch sat in the middle, gripped the handle and tapped the brush at the back. Jet leaped on to the broomstick and it whooshed through the cottage, out through the back door and into the snowy garden.

The witch looked round and smiled at the kitten.

"Would you like to go higher?" she asked.

Jet nodded and the witch nodded back.

"Hold on tight!" she said, and took the broomstick straight up into a sky filled with bright shining stars that twinkled all around them. The moon was full and the rooftops, trees and hills were all cloaked in a soft snowy blanket that shone with a magical blue light.

As he looked at the winter wonderland below, the snow began to fall again, swirling and drifting over the village. Jet peered down and spotted the people he had met throughout the day. They were all waving up to them cheerfully, and as the witch stroked his head, he recalled his mother's parting words.

"When you find your perfect human,

you'll know that's where you belong," she had said.

Jet hopped on to the witch's shoulder, brushed his head against her cheek and knew that he was home.

SEAL SONG

Julia Green

Solly crunched over the pebbles at the top of the beach, and ran across the white sand closer to the sea. The wind blew strong and the air felt cold as ice. Solly didn't mind. She loved the beach in wintertime. She skipped stones and dodged the waves that spread like lace up the beach. She laughed and danced, and did three happy cartwheels in a row.

She searched for treasure washed up by the tide after the first big winter storm. There! She pounced on a creamy-white shell with shiny mother-of-pearl inside. She picked up pretty cowrie shells for necklaces and bracelets, and filled her coat pockets with pebbles shaped perfectly for making into curled cats, or puffins, or seals. Solly and Mum would sell the shell necklaces and painted pebbles to holiday visitors next summer.

Solly sang to herself as she went along. She sang the songs her mother hummed to her when they were out in the bay, catching fish for supper, or at bedtime, to soothe her to sleep. It was much too wild and stormy to go out in their little boat today. The wind caught the words of Solly's songs about fishes and boats and seals, and tossed them in the air like seagulls.

She stopped for a moment, to look out to sea. Were there any seals out in the bay today?

Solly and her mum loved the seals.
Sometimes they fed scraps of fish to the ones
that followed their little wooden boat into
the harbour. Solly didn't like catching the
fish herself, but she loved going out in the
small boat and learning how to spot where
a shoal of mackerel were swimming strong,
by watching where the seabirds dived.

Solly searched for any signs of seals.
The waves bashed the rocks out in the bay
and sent up clouds of white foam. The tops
of the waves were white, running in like

white horses. It was much too rough today, even for seals.

Solly turned away from the sea. She looked back at their small stone house at the top of the beach. Mum was at the door, waving at her to come home.

Solly zig-zagged back along the sand and up the pebbly part of the beach to their home. Light spilled out of the windows and the open door. The house looked like a lantern, shining out into the dusk. It got dark so early in wintertime.

"Look what I found!" Solly tipped out her pockets and spread her treasures on the kitchen table for Mum to see.

Mum picked up each shell in turn. "Beautiful," she said. "Well done, Solly. We can thread these on coloured string later."

She stroked the pebbles. "We will give these eyes and noses and whiskers." In her imagination, Solly saw the smooth grey pebbles turn into seals.

Mum ladled soup into bowls. "Now come and warm up. I've lit a fire in the stove. The wind's getting up again."

The wind rattled the windows, crept through every gap and chink, and made Solly and Mum shiver, even when they sat close to the peat stove. At high tide, the waves lashed the beach and sounded so loud that Solly was scared.

"What if the sea comes right up to the house?" she asked Mum.

"There's no need to worry," Mum said.

"This little house has stayed safe and dry through many gales and tides. Come away from the window and help me paint the pebbles."

Mum and Solly sang songs together as they painted the pebbles into creatures. They sang about the lights in the harbour as the boats sail out to sea. Mum sang a lullaby about a mother and a child.

Solly sang her favourite song about a seal. On a grey pebble she painted two eyes, round and dark, and a nose and whiskers and held it up for Mum to admire.

"Beautiful," Mum said.

At last the wind dropped, the sky cleared and a huge moon rose above the sea.

Solly pressed her face against the cold window-glass. "Look at the full moon, Mum!"

The sea was calmer now. The light made a silver path across the water and cast shadows on the sand.

"Can we go outside?" Solly asked. "Please, Mum?"

Mum smiled. "Just for a little while."

They put on thick coats and scarves, and pushed their feet into wool-lined boots.

Solly opened the door. She ran outside. She spun in circles with her arms out, dancing in the magic moonlight. She stopped, and for a moment the world kept spinning.

Mum's face was touched with silver. Her eyes shone. Her breath made puffs of smoke on the cold air as she followed Solly. They played at being wild horses, puffing hot breath as they trotted along the shore.

The gale had brought new treasures. They stuffed their pockets with gleaming shells, twists of purple seaweed, turquoise string from a fishing net.

Solly galloped ahead. She left Mum far behind.

She stopped short. What was that?

Something else had been washed up, something much bigger than shells or pebbles. For a second she thought it was part of a boat, upturned on the sand.

But no. Now she was close enough to see what the storm had brought her.

"Oh!" Solly gasped.

A young seal lay on the sand. It was small, not much more than a baby.

For a horrible moment, Solly thought it was dead. Her eyes filled with tears.

But the seal opened its dark eyes and snuffled its nose.

Solly saw how scared it was. "It's OK," she whispered. "I won't hurt you."

The seal tried to roll away, but it couldn't move.

Solly saw why, now. The seal was caught in the strong strands of a torn fishing net. In all its twisting and turning to try to escape, the seal had wound itself tighter and tighter.

Solly kept her voice calm and gentle. "It's all right," she told the baby seal. "We'll help you, Mum and me. We will set you free." She crouched down and stretched out her hand, but the seal pup cried out in terror.

Solly stepped back.

She needed a knife or scissors, or something, to cut the net away. And how could she get close enough to the seal without frightening it even more?

Mum caught her up. "Poor little thing. Don't touch it," she told Solly. "A seal bite can be really nasty."

"It's so scared," Solly said. She began to sing, very softly, just like Mum had sung to her in the storm, when she was frightened of the waves. She sang a song of love and comfort, about a mother and child.

The seal pup stopped struggling.

It closed its eyes.

"Keep singing," Mum said softly to Solly. From her pocket she took out her penknife with the mother-of-pearl handle. She edged forwards.

Solly sang a song about stars.

The seal lay quietly now, as if it was fast asleep.

Mum sawed through the tough mesh very carefully so as not to hurt the seal.

Solly kept singing, soft and low, a lullaby.

Mum cut the last strand of net. The seal was free.

Solly stopped singing. In the moonlight she could see the beautiful dappled grey of the seal's furry skin. It rolled over, opened its eyes and yawned, as if it was waking from a dream.

Solly held her breath. She longed to

touch the seal, but she knew she mustn't.

A ripple of movement ran down the seal's back. It stretched, trying out its muscles. It raised its head and flippers and began an awkward rock and shuffle down the beach towards the sea.

Solly slid her cold hand into her mother's. She watched the seal pup slip into the water. Now it was free of the land, it seemed to change. It became sleek and fast. It twisted and turned in the water. For a moment it stopped and looked back at Solly with its big eyes, as if it was saying thank you. And then it turned again and swam out deeper into the moonlit waves. It dived and disappeared from view.

Solly watched and watched, hoping for one last glimpse, but the seal had gone.

"It was so lucky we were here," Solly said.

"Yes," Mum said.

Solly yawned. She was so tired now.

"Home to bed?" Mum said.

Solly nodded.

"You saved its life," Solly said as they

walked back together along the sand.

"You, too," Mum said. "You kept the seal pup calm with your lovely singing."

"Yes," Solly said. "I did." The thought gave her a warm glow, deep inside.

At home they pulled off their coats and boots, and unwound their scarves. The house was warm. The peat fire still glowed in the stove.

Solly put on her pyjamas and climbed into bed.

Mum smoothed Solly's wild hair, still damp from the night air. She kissed her goodnight and tucked her under the covers.

Mum went to the window.

"What can you see?" Solly mumbled, nearly asleep.

"The dark sea and the starlit sky," Mum said. She sang a new lullaby, about a seal girl and a seal mother.

Solly listened. She imagined the seal pup, swimming out to sea under the moon and stars, finding its way back to its mother at last.

And very soon, she was fast asleep and dreaming.

BAA HUMBUG!

Jeanne Willis

It was late December. In a faraway field at the edge of the forest, the crows were cawing, the squirrels were chattering and the rabbits were hopping up and down in great excitement. They had seen the sheep gathered in a big woolly circle under the Meeting Tree and that could only mean one thing – it was almost time for the Wild Winter Party.

It happened every Christmas and no one was more excited than Littlest Lamb. He'd never been to the party before and he listened eagerly as the rest of the flock made suggestions for the feast, fun and games. This year promised to be the best party ever – at least it did until Wolf arrived.

Wolf lived in a cave in the deepest, darkest part of the forest and he always kept himself to himself, but when he overheard the birds tweeting about the party, it sounded such fun.

Littlest Lamb was sitting with Mother Ewe as she wrote the invitations under the Meeting Tree. When Wolf appeared, Lamb almost jumped out of his skin. He had never met a wolf before and nor had any of his flock, but they had all heard terrible stories.

Mother Ewe pretended not to be frightened, but Littlest Lamb jumped down and hid behind her. Wolf looked even scarier than he had ever imagined.

"Those invitations look pretty," said Wolf. "Is one of them for me?"

Mother Ewe had written invitations for all the birds and all the beasts, but she had not written one for him.

"No!" she said. "You are not invited. Wolves are big and bad! You will frighten all the guests."

Wolf frowned. "I promise to be good," he said.

"Baa Humbug!" bleated Mother Ewe. "I don't believe you. I have never heard a story about a good wolf. Every sheep knows that all wolves are bad. Now run along and leave us alone!"

Wolf howled and ran back into the forest with his tail between his legs.

"Thank goodness he's gone," said Mother Ewe. "Now we can get on with these invitations."

Littlest Lamb came out of hiding and helped his mother by licking the envelopes.

But the next day, after the party invitations had been posted to every creature in the forest except one, Wolf came back.

Mother Ewe and Littlest Lamb were just discussing the party food when he came skulking out of the forest. His teeth looked so sharp, that Littlest Lamb hid behind the menu.

"Clover Jelly and Thistle Tarts? Mmmmmm!" said Wolf. "Please may I come to the Wild Winter Party and share your food?"

"Certainly not!" said Mother Ewe. "Every sheep knows that wolves are greedy. You'll gobble everything up."

The wolf scowled. "I promise to share," he said.

"Baa Humbug!" bleated Mother Ewe. "I have never heard a story about a wolf sharing. Be off with you!"

Before the wolf could say another word, Father Ram bustled over. He lowered his horns and chased Wolf back into the forest.

"Thank goodness he's gone!" said Mother Ewe. "Now we can bake the Christmas cake in peace."

Littlest Lamb came out of hiding and helped his mother stir the cake mixture, but as he licked the spoon, he couldn't help wondering if the stories about all wolves being bad were true. Wolf had promised to be good and he had promised to share. Maybe he really was a good wolf, in which case it didn't seem fair that he hadn't been invited to the party.

By Christmas Eve, the preparations were coming along perfectly. Littlest Lamb's brothers and sisters were busy making decorations out of fir cones. His aunts and uncles were cutting the grass to put in the sandwiches and while his cousins made the party hats, Grandma Ewe and Grandpa Ram arranged hundreds of glow-worms on the frosty branches of the Christmas Tree that twinkled like fairy lights.

Littlest Lamb watched in amazement as the bare, snowy field was transformed into a festive wonderland. There was only one more sleep until the big day.

But that afternoon, Wolf came back!

Littlest Lamb was helping Mother Ewe wrap a gift for a game of Pass the Parcel when Wolf came huffing and puffing out of the deep, dark forest towards them.

"Ooh! I've always wanted to play Pass the Parcel," he said.

Littlest Lamb was so surprised, he forgot to hide. In all the stories he'd heard about wolves, they never played Pass the Parcel – they played mean tricks. But maybe *this* wolf was different.

"May I come to the party and join in with your games?" asked Wolf.

"No!" said Mother Ewe. "Wolves are sly! Wolves cheat! It says so in all the stories. You cannot join in."

Wolf held out his paw. "I promise to play

nicely," he said. "Please give me a chance!"

"Baa Humbug!" bleated Mother Ewe. "Wolves are big, bad, greedy and sly. They always have been and always will be. You are not welcome at the Wild Winter Party. Go away and don't come back!"

Wolf threw back his head and howled. "At least let me join in with the carols at the end!" he begged.

This time, Mother Ewe was afraid that he would not take "No!" for an answer, so she called over Father Ram and all his sons and all his brothers, nephews and uncles. They lowered their horns and chased Wolf back into the forest.

"Thank goodness he's gone," said Mother Ewe. "At last, we will be able to relax and enjoy ourselves."

Christmas Day came and everything was almost ready for the party. There was only one thing missing.

"Bother! I've forgotten the holly to go on top of the pudding!" said Mother Ewe. "Be a lamb and fetch me some," she said to her littlest.

Littlest Lamb did as he was told and trotted off. At first, he could not find any holly, but as he went deeper and deeper into the forest, he found a bush with fat, red berries growing near a cave. He was about to pick some when he heard the most pitiful sound. He peeked into the cave and there was Wolf!

Littlest Lamb was so shocked, his wool

stood on end. But when he saw Wolf lying there with his head on his paws, whimpering as if his heart would break, Littlest Lamb could not help feeling sorry for him.

"Wolf, why are you crying?" he asked.

Wolf lifted his great, grizzly head and gazed mournfully at Littlest Lamb.

"I am the only one who hasn't been invited to the party!" he sobbed. "Why does everybody hate me?"

"They're afraid of you," said Littlest Lamb. "They have been told that all wolves are big and bad, and that is what they believe."

Wolf gave a deep sigh.

"That's just a fairy story," he said. "Not *all* wolves are big and bad. I'm a good wolf, but how can I prove it if no one will give me a chance?"

Littlest Lamb thought about it. Maybe Wolf was telling the truth. He had never done anything bad as far as he knew. He had always been polite and he had never hurt any of the sheep, so perhaps they were wrong about him. Littlest Lamb couldn't bear to think of Wolf spending Christmas alone, so despite everything he'd been told about wolves, he decided to trust him.

"You may come to the party if you promise to be good," he said.

Wolf stopped sobbing and smiled a big smile.

"I promise from the bottom of my heart!" he said, but then his face fell. "But what will the rest of the flock say when they see me?"

Littlest Lamb smiled.

"Not all sheep are silly," he said. "That's just a fairy story, too. I'm sure they won't mind you coming when they see how good you are."

"I hope so," said Wolf, but he didn't look very sure.

"See you at the feast!" called Littlest Lamb, and he hurried home with the sprig of holly.

That evening, as the full moon rose, the guests began to arrive. Robin came, along with Hedgehog, Weasel, Vole, Mole and

Rabbit. Squirrel, Deer and Badger came. Sleepy Dormouse and wide-awake Owl came, but there was no sign of Wolf.

He is sure to turn up soon, thought Littlest Lamb.

The feast began, but still Wolf did not arrive. The Littlest Lamb wondered why. He had wanted to come to the party so much, he had promised to be good. Suddenly, Littlest Lamb had a terrible thought. What if Wolf had not come because he knew he could not keep his promise? Maybe Mother Ewe was right and all wolves *were* bad.

Just then, Father Christmas arrived, wearing a long, red cloak and a white beard that almost touched the ground.

"Ho! Ho! Ho! Season's Bleatings, everybody!" he said.

He joined in with the feast and Littlest Lamb was so excited to see him, he forgot about Wolf for a while and tucked into the thistle tarts.

"Thank goodness we didn't invite Wolf," said Father Ram. "There would have been no food left for Father Christmas!"

Littlest Lamb said nothing, but as he helped himself to another quince pie, he hoped Wolf wasn't going hungry.

After the feast, the party games began. They played Hide-and-Squeak, Hunt the Hazelnut and Ewes-ical Bumps. Father Christmas joined in and when he won Pass the Parcel, he refused to keep the prize and gave it to Mother Ewe.

"Thank you!" she said. "I'm glad we didn't invite Wolf. He would have ruined our games."

Littlest Lamb said nothing, but he hoped Wolf wasn't too bored and lonely in his cave.

After the games, it was time for Father Christmas to give out the presents from his sack. He gave Squirrel a teasel brush to groom her fluffy tail. Hedgehog had a chestnut-case hat to keep his head warm and Mole had a beautiful necklace made from snowberries. Everyone was delighted with their gifts, but Father Christmas saved the best present for Littlest Lamb – a pair of furry slippers with matching mittens to keep his hooves warm.

"Thank you!" said Littlest Lamb. "They're just what I always wanted."

"I'm glad we didn't invite Wolf," said Grandma Ewe. "Only good creatures get gifts and everyone knows that wolves are bad."

Littlest Lamb was about to agree with her, but as Father Christmas picked up his empty sack and turned to leave, Littlest Lamb spotted a familiar grey tail poking out from underneath his long, red robe.

"It's the wolf!" he cried out.

Wolf had been at the party in disguise all along! Littlest Lamb was delighted to see him, but the rest of the guests were not. As the rams lowered their horns and surrounded him, Mother Ewe glared angrily at the other animals.

"Who invited the big bad wolf?" she demanded.

This time, Littlest Lamb spoke up.

"It was me," he said. "I invited him. He is a *good* wolf! He made me a promise and he kept it. He shared our food, he played nicely and he gave each of us a lovely gift."

Everyone at the party fell silent. They gazed at Wolf in his Father Christmas outfit and thought about what Littlest Lamb had said. The wolf had been kind and generous to everyone and they felt ashamed for believing all the horrid stories they had heard about him.

"Littlest Lamb is right," said Mother Ewe. "I am sorry, Wolf. I was wrong to believe that you were bad just because it says so in stories. There are good wolves, too. From now on, you will *always* be invited to our Wild Winter Party."

Littlest Lamb was so happy to hear it, he skipped up and down. But suddenly, he realized something that made his tail droop.

"Wolf is the only one without a gift and he has been *very, very* good," he whispered to Mother Ewe. But even though Littlest Lamb spoke very softly, Wolf heard every word.

"Littlest Lamb," he said, "you have already given me the greatest gift I could ever wish for – Christmas with friends!"

And no matter what the fairy stories may say, when the church bells struck twelve on that magical, moonlit night, the faraway field filled with the sweet sound of an animal choir singing in perfect harmony, with a wolf leading the carols.

THE NATIVITY
PARADE

Katy Cannon

Holly stood on the kitchen chair and tried not to fidget as her mum pinned up the shiny blue robe.

"Just a few more…" Mum muttered, grabbing another pin from the sewing box. "We don't want you tripping over in the parade now, do we?"

Every December, Holly's village held a special procession, telling the story of baby Jesus's birth. Children from the local primary school all wore costumes and walked through the streets to a pretend stable outside the church. There, they took their places in the nativity scene – a living picture of the stable in Bethlehem on the first ever Christmas night.

The Nativity Parade was one of Holly's favourite things about Christmas and this year it would be even more special. She was going to be dressed in a blue robe and riding a real-life donkey, because…

"I can't believe I'm going to be Mary!" Holly whispered, for the hundredth time since Mrs Finnegan told her that she had the part.

Mum smiled, adding another pin. "You'll be brilliant. I can't wait to come and watch."

"And Harley," Holly said anxiously. "Harley can come and watch, too, right?"

Harley must have heard his name because he came bounding into the kitchen, barking with excitement. Holly's Irish wolfhound was her best friend in the whole wide world. She loved coming up with new games for the two of them to play. When he'd first arrived, Harley had been quite small, but now at one year old, he was almost taller than her!

Holly grinned as Harley ducked under the kitchen table to get to her. His big head bumped against the underside of the table, then his body crashed into the chair she was standing on, making it rock.

"Harley!" Holly cried, grabbing on to the back of the chair to help her stay upright. "Sit! Sit, Harley!"

She had spent the last year working really hard on training Harley and as soon as she said "Sit!" he did exactly as he was told. But Harley obeyed so enthusiastically that, when he sat, one of his legs bashed into Mum's sewing box, sending pins and reels of cotton skittering across the tiled floor.

Holly winced. "Sorry, Mum. He didn't mean to. He was just—"

"Trying to get to you." Mum sighed as she gathered up the scattered sewing supplies. "I know. That's all he ever wants – to be with you. The problem is, he's a very *big* dog, and sometimes he doesn't pay a lot of attention to what's between him and you!"

Holly knew what Mum meant. That was how Mum's vase got broken. And the garden gate. Dad's roses. And quite a few other things.

"I know you really want him to see the parade, Holly," said Mum. "But I'm just not sure he'll be able to behave himself."

Holly swallowed. It was her big moment and she wanted her best friend with her. Mum gave her a hug and kissed the top of her head. "I'll tell you what. Why don't I take Harley along to your dress rehearsal tomorrow? Mrs Finnegan said she wanted a few parents to come so your class gets used to having an audience. If he can keep out of trouble then, he can come with me to watch the parade in the evening."

"Brilliant!" Holly jumped up and down

on the chair, and a couple of pins fell out of her robe.

"But first we've got to finish adjusting this costume," Mum said with a laugh. "Or Harley won't be the only thing we have to worry about at the dress rehearsal!"

The dress rehearsal was taking place at Holly's school. Several other parents were already standing round the edges of the playground when Holly, Mum and Harley arrived.

"Now remember, Harley," Holly said sternly as the Irish wolfhound sat beside Mum. "Best behaviour."

Holly waved goodbye to Mum and ran into the hall to put on her costume.

Inside, Holly's friends were all getting ready for the parade, too. Holly looked around the hall and saw Sophie, already in her angel costume, standing very still while Mrs Finnegan attached a tinsel halo to her headband. Across the way, Lexie wriggled into her sheep costume. Over at the costume cupboard, Dean and Callum had found two donkey-ear headbands and were braying and hee-hawing, while all the other children laughed!

"Boys!" Mrs Finnegan called, but she was laughing, too. "We already have a donkey, remember? Daisy from Buttercup Farm will be there this evening for Holly to ride in the parade. We are missing a couple of shepherds, though…" She looked pointedly at the two costumes sitting on the side, and Dean and Callum hurried to put them on.

Holly took her robe out of her bag. She tugged it over her head and pushed her arms through the sleeves. Then she pulled out the white cloth, ready for Mrs Finnegan to help her put it on her head.

Holly's tummy felt like it was full of butterflies, but she was more nervous about Harley behaving than she was about taking part in the parade!

Finally, they were all ready. Mrs Finnegan led the children out into the playground and they lined up in their correct order. Later, they would be walking half a mile through the village to the church, but for the rehearsal, cones had been set out in a winding path across the playground. At the front of the line was the star – Holly's friend Emilia, dressed all in silver and holding a huge, glittery cardboard star on a wooden stick. Next came the angels, then the shepherds and the sheep, then the wise men and the camels. Last of all came Kai playing Joseph and Holly playing Mary. Tonight, Daisy the donkey would be there, too, but for now they were practising without her. It would be the first time they'd ever had a real live animal in the parade!

Holly's friend Callum had pointed out that the wise men should come last, because they didn't arrive until Epiphany – he knew, because it was his brother's birthday – but Mrs Finnegan had decided that it would be best if the donkey came last for the parade, in case of accidents.

Mrs Finnegan clapped her hands. "Now, everyone remember – walk slowly and calmly, following the cones. And if we're all ready … begin!"

Holly glanced across at Harley as they started to move. He was still sitting nicely beside Mum. But as the shepherds and the sheep paraded past him, Harley let out a loud, excited bark. One of the shepherds turned to look at the big dog, and the children behind crashed into him, causing a shepherd pile-up.

"Stop!" Mrs Finnegan called out. "We'll have to start again."

Holly watched as Mum tugged Harley a little further back, right to the edge of the playground. Had Harley been looking for her, Holly wondered? That was usually why he started barking or got excited.

"OK, shepherds, off you go!"

The line of children started moving again, but as the angels set off, Holly saw Harley stand up – he had spotted her! He started barking again and strained at his lead, pulling Mum forwards a few steps – just far enough that he almost tripped up Angel Gabriel!

Mrs Finnegan called another halt. Holly sighed. There was no way Mum would let Harley come to the real parade if he couldn't even manage to sit through the dress rehearsal. Holly knew he'd be as good as gold if he could be next to her in the line, but there weren't any Irish wolfhounds in the nativity story.

"Sorry!" Mum called as she and Harley moved even further away, almost past the playground gate. This time, the parade went smoothly.

"And now take your places in the stable," Mrs Finnegan said, pointing to the cones laid out to show where the stable would be. "Just like we practised."

Holly took her place, grinning. Harley had done it! Maybe he could come to the parade after all!

Suddenly, she heard barking. Harley was racing towards her across the playground, his lead loose and Mum chasing behind.

"Oh, Harley," Holly groaned. But there was nothing she could do to stop the one-year-old Irish wolfhound in full chase.

Harley crashed through the crowd of children, sending the manger flying. He jumped up to greet Holly, putting his giant paws on her shoulders. Holly cuddled him.

"Why couldn't you just sit and watch?" Holly whispered into Harley's fur, but she already knew the answer. "You just wanted to join in, didn't you, boy? You wanted to be with me." But now he wouldn't be there for the performance at all. Mum would have to take Harley home. They'd blown their only chance. It was supposed to be Holly's big day, but now she just felt like crying.

The parade route started just outside the school gates. By the time they were ready to begin, it was dark outside, and the candle lamps that lined the path through the village were already lit. Holly stared at all the people in amazement. She'd never known the village to be so busy! This year's parade was bigger than ever, with even a few stalls selling food and decorations lining the parade route. The church choir were singing carols, and other villagers were handing out cups of hot chocolate to the crowds.

Holly was so excited to be part of the parade, and to be looking after Daisy the donkey – but she still couldn't stop thinking about how Harley was going to miss it. She stood on her tiptoes to try and spot Mrs Finnegan over the crowd. Her teacher had gone to fetch Daisy from the farmer, who was bringing her into the village from Buttercup Farm.

Mrs Finnegan's head popped into view through the crowd, and Holly peered closer to see Daisy. Where was she?

"I'm so sorry, Holly," Mrs Finnegan said, as she reached her. She clapped her hands. "Everyone! Listen, please. I'm afraid that Daisy the donkey is sick, and won't be able to take part in the parade tonight after all."

Holly's heart sank even lower. Everything was going wrong today!

"I know it'll be a shame to have the nativity without a donkey," Mrs Finnegan said. "But I am certain you'll all do a brilliant job anyway! I'm so excited to see you parade through the village."

Without a donkey, and without Harley.

Unless… Suddenly, Holly remembered the donkey ears that Dean and Callum had found at school. An idea started to form in her mind. A brilliant idea that made her grin brighter than the lamplight.

"Don't worry," she told Mrs Finnegan. "I know what we can do." She whispered her idea to the teacher, who looked uncertain.

"Are you sure?" Mrs Finnegan asked. "Harley's a very … excitable dog."

"Please, Mrs Finnegan," Holly said. "I know he can do it."

Mrs Finnegan stared at Holly for a long moment before she nodded. "Then we'd better call your mum!"

Finally, the Nativity Parade began winding through the streets. First came the star, Emilia's costume glittering. Next, the angels, then the shepherds and their sheep, the wise men and their camels, Joseph and then, right at the back came a beaming Holly.

Instead of riding on a donkey, Holly held a lead in her hand. And beside her walked a perfectly behaved Harley, with a donkey-ears headband perched on his head. Now that Harley was beside Holly, he didn't need to run anywhere.

Holly's heart swelled with pride as they walked through the village. Harley had proved to everyone that he *could* be a good dog. Although perhaps Holly might have to work on training him to stay with other people before next year's parade!

The crowd applauded as they walked past in the candlelight. It was the best Nativity Parade ever!

OLA TO THE
RESCUE!

Tracey Corderoy

Ola, the little polar bear, was making a
snowman with her best friend, Wilbur
Walrus, when her big brothers and sister
appeared.

Ola frowned. Tomorrow Jack, Belle
and the twins would be performing in
the annual ice-dancing competition. This
morning they'd been practising on the big
frozen lake. But Ola couldn't think why
they'd be heading back already.

As they came closer, Ola then saw that
her big sister, Belle, was all shivery.

"Belle's caught a cold," sighed big brother,

Jack. The twins, George and Max, nodded.

"I need to go to bed," sniffed Belle. "Achoo!"

Ola left Wilbur with her brothers and took Belle into their cave. She tucked her up under a big cosy blanket.

"I hope you feel better soon, Belle," Ola whispered.

Back outside, Ola found Wilbur and her brothers in their ice-den down the garden. Ola's brothers looked sad.

"What's wrong?" asked Ola.

George shook his head. "The ice-dancing competition…"

Ola's brothers and sister took part every year. They'd been working on their ice-dance for weeks. They always asked Ola if she wanted to join in, but each time Ola said she'd prefer to watch.

"What are we going to do?" Jack groaned. "The competition's *tomorrow*. There's no way Belle will be better by then."

"Why not just leave Belle's part out?" suggested Wilbur.

"We can't do that!" Max cried.

"Belle's part is very important," agreed Jack. "The dance tells a story. I'm Brightpaw – king of the woodland sprites. And it's *my* job to make the wood sparkle with frost."

"But me and Max are fog goblins," said George. "We like everything to be gloomy."

"So there's a battle between us," Max went on. "With tons of really cool stunts. Bright-paw's losing the battle, when suddenly he sees a *shooting star*. He wishes on it, gets special powers and defeats the fog goblins once and for all."

"But Bright-paw won't be able to defeat the goblins without the shooting star," sighed George. "Which was *Belle*'s part."

Jack looked at Ola thoughtfully.

"Hey – you could do Belle's part!"

"Me? Be the shooting star?" Ola gasped.

She did want to help her brothers out, but ice-skating meant slipping and sliding and falling flat on her nose...

Ola shook her head. "I can't!" she gulped.

"But we *need* you," pleaded Max. "The snow hares have a brilliant dance. And the arctic foxes *and* the reindeer are going to be competing, too."

"No — s-sorry, I just can't!" cried Ola, dashing out of the den.

"Ola!" called Wilbur. "Wait!" And he hurried out after her.

Wilbur looked around the garden. There was no sign of Ola as big fluffy snowflakes tumbled out of a dark grey sky. Poor Ola! Wilbur had never seen her so upset.

Wilbur followed Ola's pawprints in the snow and finally found her in a rocky hollow. She was staring out at the big icebergs floating in the clear blue sea. In the distance snow-capped mountains reached to the sky.

"Are you OK, Ola?" Wilbur asked, sitting down beside her. Still looking out to sea, Ola nodded back.

"I'm just too scared of ice-skating," she said, her breath misty and white. "I tried it once when I was really little. I fell flat on my nose. And it hurt! A family of arctic foxes saw me and started laughing…"

"Don't worry, Ola!" Wilbur said quickly. "We're all sacred of something. Even me."

"Even *you*?" Ola looked at him and Wilbur nodded.

"I'm scared of water. Well, swimming!" he said. He gazed out at the icy water and shuddered. "But just because something's frightening, doesn't mean we shouldn't try it. So, do you want to try ice-skating again?"

Ola thought. She really did want to help her brothers. And ice-skating might not be quite as scary with Wilbur holding her paw. But she'd never know for sure unless she tried…

"All right," said Ola finally. "If you'll help, I'll try again."

"Great!" Wilbur smiled. "I know just the place for beginners!"

Wilbur led Ola to a small frozen pond and they started by simply stepping on to the ice.

"Whoa!" gulped Ola, grabbing Wilbur's flipper.

The ice under Ola's feet was so cold that she felt it burn her paws. And suddenly the soft, gentle breeze seemed to roar like a giant.

"I don't like it!" Ola was trembling.

"It's OK!" said Wilbur. "I won't let go."

When Ola was ready, they tried to glide. Slowly at first. Then a little bit faster. Then a little bit faster still. Each time Ola wobbled, her tummy lurched like a snowflake tossed in a storm. Ola could hardly breathe, it was so scary!

They practised all through lunchtime. All through teatime, too. And finally Ola was *skating*, just a bit.

But then it happened. Ola lost concentration and one paw slid out too wide.

"Ah!" she cried, and down she tumbled— "Ow!"

"Oh no! Are you all right?" Wilbur quickly helped her up.

"Silly old ice!" said Ola with a frown.

She rubbed her nose where she'd bumped it. But to her surprise, the nasty sting was already fading away. And Wilbur hadn't laughed at all…

Ola felt braver. She could do this! So she stepped out on to the ice again, all by herself.

"Woooo-oooo," she squeaked, her legs as stiff as tree trunks and her movements slow and jerky.

"Look – you're *doing* it!" Wilbur clapped excitedly. "You're skating all by yourself!"

"I am! I really am!" Ola cried.

Ola and Wilbur were still at the pond when the sky turned from grey to a deep inky blue and tiny stars started peeping out. Ola still felt shaky on the ice but she was much better than before. In the magical moonlight, she even managed a *smile*...

"Hey, Wilbur," said Ola finally. "I am going to skate in the competition tomorrow. Everybody's worked really hard and I don't want to let them down."

Wilbur smiled, a big curly-whiskered smile. "Yippee!"

"Wilbur, thanks for your help!" Ola called as she set off home to tell her brothers. "You were right about trying, you know."

Looking suddenly thoughtful, Wilbur waved back.

"See you tomorrow, Ola!"

The next morning, right after breakfast, Ola put on her shooting-star costume. "Oh!" she gasped, looking down at the sparkles. It was beautiful!

A tiara of stars made from icicles twinkled on her head, and her star beams were long silver ribbons threaded with snowflakes.

Ola's brothers were over the moon that she had decided to skate. Even though – as she'd told them a million times – she was still ever so wobbly.

"I wish I had more time to practise," she said. She hadn't even skated on the big frozen lake. It was bound to be harder than the pond.

"I'm sure you'll be OK!" Jack smiled.

But Ola wasn't sure. Not at all. Suddenly her tummy was turning somersaults!

"Come on!" called the twins. Already it was time to go.

Although Ola loved her costume, she couldn't help but still feel nervous. Especially when she got to the big frozen lake and saw how many animals had come to watch the competition. There were arctic foxes, seals, snow hares, reindeer, polar bears and walruses. But not one of the walruses, Ola saw, was Wilbur. Where could her best friend be?

Ola's toes tingled and her heart thumped hard as she glanced up at her brothers. All three of them looked so excited. They had waited for this all year. Ola swallowed hard. Just one careless stumble would ruin all their hard work...

The reindeer were the first to dance. But they were so nervous they went too fast. Then two pairs of tangled antlers sent the whole team crashing down.

"Oooh!" gasped the crowd as the reindeer plodded off glumly.

Next came the arctic foxes. But although their costumes were beautiful, their dance was very gloomy, so Ola felt almost sure *they* wouldn't win!

The snow hares followed with a toy-box dance. They twirled and spun gracefully, like little ballerinas. Their white fur twinkled in the morning light and no one put a paw wrong.

"Hooray!" cheered the crowd. And now it was the *polar bears'* turn...

Ola's brothers stepped on to the ice. Ola waited nervously at the side as Jack did his Bright-paw dance. Then it was George and Max's turn as the fog goblins.

So far it was going really well. The twins' somersaults were *amazing*. But Ola knew that any minute now, she would be on and there was still no sign of Wilbur. Why hadn't he come to watch?

With that, she spotted a little walrus across the frozen lake.

"Wilbur!" Ola smiled. But her smile quickly faded and her eyes grew big and wide.

Wilbur had slipped down a fishing hole in the ice!

"Wilbur!" gasped Ola, remembering at once that Wilbur was scared of the water.

She launched herself on to the ice at once.
"I'll save you!"

Ola skated across the frozen lake as fast
as her legs would carry her. The crowd
became a blur as she zoomed along.

As soon as she reached the other side,
she leaped through the air and landed with
a *bump* right beside the fishing hole. Then
plunging in a paw, she pulled out a very
soggy Wilbur…

"Wilbur!" panted Ola. "Are you OK?"

Wilbur was smiling. "Of course!"

"But you slipped down the fishing hole!" Ola said.

"No – I *dived* down the fishing hole!" grinned Wilbur.

He told her that after she'd left last night, he'd been thinking a lot about trying.

"And I thought I should try swimming," he said. "Because you were brave and tried ice-skating. So I found a small puddle and dipped in my flipper. And guess what! It felt fine! So I dipped in my tail. Then ALL of me! And then I tried *swimming* – and I could do it! I was just going to have a quick practice on my way to watch you skate—"

"Skate!" cried Ola. She'd forgotten all about the competition.

Suddenly they heard an enormous cheer.

Ola and Wilbur skated over to Ola's brothers, who all had great big smiles on their faces.

"Ola!" cried Jack. "We won the competition!"

"Because of *you!*" George and Max beamed.

"Me?" Ola shrugged. "But I was trying to save Wilbur. I didn't do anything!"

"Oh yes, you did!" Jack nodded. "When you skated across the lake you were the fastest shooting star the judges had ever *seen* – so we won!"

Ola giggled with delight. By dashing to save Wilbur, she'd done her best skating ever!

"Three cheers for Ola!" Wilbur cried. "The very best friend in the world!"

DENZIL'S ADVENTURE

Liss Norton

Denzil Dragon was bored. There was nothing to do in his cave but play with his same old pebbles, talk to his same old parents and look at the same old walls. Outside there was nothing but boring snowy mountains and a boring blue sky. He sighed loudly. If only something exciting would happen…

"What's wrong, darling?" asked his mother. "You sound fed up."

"I *am* fed up." Denzil puffed out a flicker of flame. "Everything's so boring. Day after day, week after week… I want to do something exciting!"

His father looked up from tidying the log pile. "I felt like that when I was your age," he said, "so I set off to find adventure."

"Really?" An adventure would be thrilling, Denzil thought. "I'll do that, too!" he whooped. "I'll go right now!"

"Well, I didn't mean…" began his father, but Denzil's mind was made up.

He made some sandwiches for the journey and packed them in his rucksack.

"Be careful," said his mother.

"I will." Denzil hugged her.

"Don't stay away too long," his father said.

Denzil hugged him, too, then hurried out of the cave, spread his wings and took off. "Goodbye!" he called as he soared high.

The winter air was cold and Denzil blew a few flames to warm himself. Then he flew

up and over the top of the highest mountain and away into the distance.

He felt brave at setting off on his own and he flew strongly. The whole world lay ahead of him and he let himself imagine meeting new friends and finding an amazing place to stay for a while as he explored a new area.

The mountains ended at last and Denzil saw a huge forest below him. He swooped down eagerly. He'd never seen a forest before and he flew just above the treetops, gazing all around. The snow was less thick here, but he loved the way it clung to the leafless, winter branches and lay piled against the tree trunks.

Suddenly he saw a movement below him. Someone was there!

Denzil flew down between the branches and spotted tiny birds flitting to and fro.

"Hello," they chirped. "You're new here, aren't you? What sort of bird are you?"

"I'm not a bird, I'm a dragon," Denzil said, perching on a low branch. "My name's Denzil."

"We've never had a dragon here before," the birds twittered, settling all around him.

"I'm having an adventure," said Denzil. "This looks an exciting place. Can I stay here with you for a little while?"

"Of course you can," the birds replied. "You must build a nest." They flew off in every direction and returned a moment later carrying twigs in their beaks. "We'll show you how to do it."

Denzil was delighted. "Building a nest will be a great adventure!" he exclaimed.

The birds showed him how to weave the twigs together, but it wasn't as easy as it looked. It took Denzil hours to make his nest, even though the birds helped him.

"Perfect!" he cried, when his nest was finished. "It's just the right size for me."

The sun had set while they'd been working and now it was time for bed. Denzil settled down in his nest. "The first night of my adventure," he said with a happy sigh. He ate one of his sandwiches, then shut his eyes, ready for a good night's sleep. But the twigs were scratchy and one of them was digging into his bottom. Denzil wriggled round, trying to make himself more comfortable, but now a twig was poking him in the chest.

It began to snow. Denzil shivered as the cold flakes settled on his head and back. "Why don't nests have roofs?" he called into the darkness, but the birds were already asleep and nobody answered.

By morning Denzil had made up his mind. He'd had enough of twiggy nests. "I'm going to find an adventure somewhere else," he said.

The birds gathered round him sadly. "You will come back and visit us, won't you, Denzil?"

"Definitely. But I won't stay the night." Denzil spread his wings and took off.

He flew a long way – until the forest ended and snowy fields stretched away into the distance. His heart began to pound with excitement. He'd never seen fields before and he flew low over them, admiring their flatness and the way their snowy covering twinkled in the sunshine. They were nothing like the mountains where he'd grown up.

Flashes of movement caught his eye and he flew over to see what they were. Rabbits were chasing each other through the snow.

"Hello," called Denzil, landing near them.

The rabbits sat up on their hind legs and stared at him, their long ears twitching.

"My name's Denzil and I'm having an adventure."

Cautiously the rabbits crept towards him. "Welcome," they said.

"Where do you live?" Denzil asked. He couldn't see any caves or nests.

"Under the ground in burrows," said a bold, young rabbit.

Denzil loved the sound of that. An underground home would have a roof, and it wouldn't be made of sharp twigs. "I'd like to stay in a burrow with you for a little while," he said.

The rabbits scratched their ears thoughtfully. "Our homes are too small for you," one said. "You'll have to dig a burrow of your own, but the ground's frozen solid."

"I can fix that," said Denzil. He blew a jet of flame and a patch of snow melted.

The rabbits stared in astonishment, then they began scraping at the earth. "The ground's not frozen any more!" they cried.

With the rabbits' help, Denzil soon dug a burrow just big enough for him to squeeze into. He had to fold his wings tightly against his body, and he couldn't stretch his neck or tail, but at least the roof kept the snow off his head and back.

"Thanks for helping me," he said.

He played with the rabbits all day, and when night came he wriggled into his burrow. He ate a sandwich, then tried to sleep. But it was hard to get comfortable. There was no room to turn round and when his nose started to itch he couldn't even reach to scratch it. The night seemed endless.

When morning came at last, Denzil crawled outside. "I don't think a burrow's the best place for a dragon," he told the rabbits. "I'm going on, but I'll come back and visit you another time."

"Goodbye! Good luck!" called the rabbits.

Denzil flew on and on, searching for somewhere even more exciting than a forest or a field. At last he came to a great blanket of beautiful, glittering snow. Beyond it was a turquoise sea, dotted with rafts of floating ice. Polar bears were taking turns swimming to the rafts.

Denzil flew down eagerly and landed on some ice.

"Hello," he said. "My name's Denzil. I'm having an adventure. Please can I stay with you for a while?"

"Of course," the polar bears replied.

"We live in ice caverns," one of them told Denzil, "and there's an empty one that should suit you. Come on, I'll show you."

He padded away and Denzil followed him, slipping and sliding on the ice. Soon they reached a towering cliff. There was a large opening in the side of the cliff.

"Here we are," the polar bear said.

Denzil hurried inside and gasped in amazement. The cavern's walls and ceiling were a gorgeous silvery-blue that glittered in the light shining in through the doorway. Shimmering icicles hung from the ceiling and the floor sparkled as though it were scattered with diamonds.

"Amazing!" cried Denzil. "This is the most exciting place I've ever seen!"

He played with the polar bears all afternoon, sliding on the ice and making snow bears and snow dragons, but he was impatient for night to come. It would be lovely to sleep in the beautiful ice cavern.

The sun set at last and the polar bears headed for home.

"Goodnight," Denzil said. He hurried

to his ice cavern and ate his last sandwich, then he lay down on a handy ledge.

Before long he was shivering violently. "It's t-t-too c-c-cold," he groaned through chattering teeth. He blew a flame to warm himself up, but the heat began to melt the icicles and freezing water dripped on his head. "I can't stay here," he sighed. "An ice cavern is no good for a fire-breathing dragon."

As soon as morning came, Denzil said goodbye to his polar-bear friends. "I'll come back and visit," he called as he flew away.

Denzil flew for miles and miles. "What I want is a home that's big enough for a dragon to move about," he told himself, "with a roof, no scratchy twigs and *definitely* no ice! And, of course, it has to be somewhere exciting." He scanned the ground as he flew, but nowhere seemed quite right.

At last he reached a range of high, snowy mountains. He felt a rush of excitement as he looked at their craggy peaks and snowy hollows. What an amazing place! There were so many nooks and crannies to explore. And that steep slope would make a perfect slide. If only he could find somewhere to live nearby.

Suddenly, ahead of him, he saw a cave opening that shone with warm, yellow light. Denzil's heart thumped as he sped towards it. It looked big enough for a dragon.

He landed on the wide ledge outside the cave and saw a pile of lovely, smooth pebbles. His excitement grew. Those pebbles would be perfect for playing with.

Looking into the cave, he saw a mossy

boulder. Two dragons were sitting on it side by side. "Mum?" Denzil cried. "Dad?"

He rushed inside and hugged them. He'd had a great adventure and made lots of new friends to visit, but now he knew he'd reached the end of his journey.

"It's funny," he said as he squeezed on to the boulder between his parents, "I never knew our mountains were so exciting." Now he'd returned from his adventure, he knew he'd never be bored again.

A WINTER
RESCUE

Linda Chapman

Tabitha dragged a large branch across the path and then scrambled back on to Belle, her chestnut pony.

"Jumping time, Belle!" she said. Belle loved jumping and the woods near their house were the perfect place to practise.

"Watch this, Harry!" Tabitha called to her five-year-old brother. He was busy building a den out of branches with Rhodes the rabbit, his favourite toy.

Tabitha cantered Belle towards the branch and Belle leaped over, clearing it easily.

"Good girl!" cried Tabitha.

Belle snorted happily, her breath freezing into white clouds.

"Did you see how well Belle just jumped?" Tabitha called to Harry.

He looked up from his den. "It's only a little jump," he said, unimpressed. "Even Rhodes and I could jump that."

Tabitha frowned. "No, you couldn't."

Harry put Rhodes on his shoulders and ran at the jump. He leaped into the air but his legs were too short to clear the branch and he landed on top of it, snapping it in two.

"Oh, Harry! You've just wrecked it!" Tabitha cried crossly.

Harry picked himself up and dusted down Rhodes. He looked a bit embarrassed. "So? It was a stupid jump anyway," he said.

Tabitha glared at him. "No, it wasn't."

"It was. It was a stupid jump for a stupid pony!" Harry stomped back to his den and went inside.

Tabitha took a deep breath. Harry was so annoying! When he was a baby he'd been really cute, but ever since he'd started school, Harry had become so irritating. So far this holiday, he had left the lids off all her felt-tip pens so they dried out, tried to steal her top-secret diary and made up a silly song about her that he wouldn't stop singing. Her mum said she should just ignore him, but it was hard!

"If you're going to say things like that, I'm going back to the house," she snapped.

"But I haven't finished my den yet!" Harry protested.

"Well, you should have thought about that before you were horrible about Belle," Tabitha said. "You have to come back, too. You're not allowed to stay out here on your own."

Harry hesitated and then crawled out of the den. He trailed behind Tabitha and Belle, his hands in his pockets. "It's not fair," he whinged. "Why do we always have to do what you want?"

Tabitha ignored him. She was ready

to get back to the warm house now. Her fingers and toes were freezing despite her gloves and thick socks. *I wonder if it'll snow today*, she thought, looking up at the grey sky. *It's definitely cold enough.* She stroked Belle's thick blonde mane. She would put a warm rug on Belle when they got back to the farmyard and give her a big hay net to munch on.

Tabitha looked back to check Harry was still following. She frowned at her little brother. Something was missing… Rhodes! He wasn't in Harry's hands, which must mean he was still in the den. Should she tell Harry? She hesitated. If she told him, she knew he would make her go back to the den, but they were almost home, and it was so cold…

Harry looked up and when he caught her staring at him, he stuck out his tongue. Tabitha looked away crossly.

Rhodes can stay in the den, she thought. *Harry's not a baby, he can sleep without him for one night. It's no big deal.*

As soon as they got back to the farmyard, Harry ran inside the house. Tabitha took off Belle's tack in the stable, buckled up her rug and gave her some carrots. The pony nuzzled her and Tabitha smiled. Belle always made her feel better.

Inside, she found Harry helping her mum make some gingerbread biscuits. Christmas songs were playing and Harry was looking much more cheerful as he pressed the pastry cutters into the dough.

"Look, I'm making a biscuit for Belle!"

He beamed and pointed to a biscuit in the shape of a carrot. "I've made one for you, too, Tabs. Do you like it?" He pointed to another biscuit made with a bell-shape cutter. "It's a bell because of Belle!"

Tabitha's remaining crossness faded away. Harry might be annoying at times, but he could also be really nice.

"I do like it. Thanks, Harry. I'll make one for you, too," she said.

"Wash your hands first, Tabs," said her mum.

Tabitha made a car for Harry and then they worked together to make some star-shaped biscuits for their gran, Tabitha rolling out the squishy dough and Harry cutting out the shapes.

"We can take some round to the

Haywards later," Mum said as she took a tray of biscuits out of the oven.

Tabitha looked up. "Have they found Poppy yet?" Mr and Mrs Hayward were their next-door neighbours and Poppy was their black-and-white cat. She had gone missing a few days ago.

"No, she's still missing," Mum said. "The Haywards are very worried about her. She's due to have her kittens any day."

Tabitha bit her lip. "I really hope she comes home soon." Whenever Tabitha went round to the Haywards' house, Poppy would press against her legs, purring. *Poor Poppy*, Tabitha thought. *It's so cold outside, I hope she's all right!*

Harry scraped up the last few bits of biscuit dough. "I'm going to make a biscuit for Rhodes now," he announced.

Guilt flared up inside Tabitha. Rhodes! He was still in the den. *What's going to happen when Harry goes to bed and he realizes Rhodes isn't here?* she thought. *He'll be so upset!* She swallowed. Glancing across the table, she saw Harry carefully cutting out a rabbit shape…

"I'm just going to go and see Belle," she said suddenly.

Pulling on her coat and boots, Tabitha ran to Belle's stable. *I have to get Rhodes,* she thought. Belle looked slightly surprised as Tabitha removed her rug, but she didn't object.

"We've got a rabbit to rescue," Tabitha whispered as she put the bridle on. Not bothering with the saddle, she led Belle out of the stable and scrambled on to her back. A few flakes of snow swirled down from the dark sky. "Let's go, girl!" Tabitha said.

She and Belle cantered up the path, but as they rode further away from the brightly lit farmyard, it became harder to see. The clouds were blocking out the moon and stars. Tabitha peered through the darkness, her heart beating fast. She'd never liked riding at night. She knew it was silly, but

she always imagined monsters hiding in the shadows. Stroking Belle's neck, she tried to be brave. *I'm with Belle,* she thought, taking a deep breath. *I'll be OK.*

She kicked Belle on and the pony responded eagerly. As they entered the woods, the moon finally came out from behind a cloud, lighting up the pile of branches that was Harry's den. *Now, all I need to do is get Rhodes and then we can go back,* thought Tabitha. She was just about to dismount when the branches of the den suddenly moved!

Tabitha froze. What was that?

The branches shifted again. Fear rushed through Tabitha. Maybe it *was* a monster! She forgot all about finding Rhodes and tried to pull Belle's head round towards home, but Belle refused to turn.

"What are you doing, Belle? Come on!" Tabitha pleaded.

Belle ignored her. She stretched her muzzle towards the den, her nostrils blowing in and out.

"No, Belle!" Tabitha gasped, pulling frantically on the reins.

Stepping forwards, Belle pushed at the branches with her nose. There was a small, weak mew.

A cat!

Her fear fading as quickly as it had flared up, Tabitha threw herself off Belle. Pulling the branches apart gently she peered inside. Could it be…?

Yes!

There was Rhodes propped up against a

branch and there, next to him, was a black-and-white cat, stretched out on her side with four newborn kittens snuggling into her fur.

"Oh, wow!" breathed Tabitha, relief swamping her. "Poppy! You've had your kittens!"

Poppy mewed anxiously again. Tabitha shrugged off her coat and draped it over

Poppy's back, being careful not to touch the kittens. She knew mother animals could be very protective of their babies, but Poppy seemed to understand that she was trying to help and didn't hiss or move away.

"We've all been so worried about you," Tabitha murmured. "Have you been looking for somewhere quiet to have your kittens all this time? I guess you must have sneaked into the den after we left. I'll go and get Mum. She'll know what to do."

She used a tree stump to climb on to Belle's back and they galloped home through the snow.

"I can't believe Poppy was so lucky!" Mrs Hayward said, a few hours later. "If Tabitha

hadn't been out in the woods, we might not have found her until it was too late."

Poppy and her newborn kittens were now lying inside a cardboard box in front of the radiator in the Haywards' living room. Mr and Mrs Hayward had headed straight out to rescue Poppy when Tabitha's mum had called.

"It's snowing so heavily now," said Tabitha's mum. "If the kittens had been out there overnight they might have died."

"But they didn't because Tabitha and Belle rescued them," said Harry. "And they rescued Rhodes, too." He hugged his rabbit tightly. "Everyone's safely home for Christmas."

"Belle was amazing," said Tabitha. "I think she knew it was Poppy in the den."

"Belle's really clever," Harry agreed. "I'm

sorry I said she was stupid – I'll never say it again."

Tabitha smiled at him – he wasn't such a bad brother really.

Her mum shook her head at her. "You know, I'm still not happy you went to the woods alone in the dark, although it *was* very brave of you."

Tabitha smiled. "I wasn't alone, I had Belle to look after me." She glanced at the door. "Can I go and see her?"

"Of course," said her mum. Her eyes twinkled. "Just no more night-time rides, OK?"

Tabitha pulled on her wellies and ran outside, crossing the Haywards' farmyard into their own. Belle whinnied softly as she saw her coming.

"Oh, Belle," Tabitha murmured. "We're going to have a really good Christmas because of you – it's lovely knowing that Poppy and her kittens are safe and warm inside. You're such a clever pony."

Belle nuzzled against her and then snorted as if to say, *I know!*

SNOWY

Lucy Courtenay

The snowflakes catching on Daisy's eyelashes felt like tiny kisses. She brushed them off her face with her mittened fingers. The snow was starting to blur the world and Daisy felt as if her garden was turning into somewhere strange and white and wild. The North Pole, maybe. She put her hands back on the rough trunk of the tree.

"Ready?" called Dad.

"Ready!" Daisy said.

"Ready!" added Daisy's little sister, Tiggy, keen not to be left out.

"One, two, three," said Dad. "Push!"

Daisy pushed. Tiggy pushed. With a creak, the freshly sawn tree pulled away from the jagged stump and fell to the ground with a whispery whoosh that made Tiggy squeal and Daisy jump back with laughter. Dad tied the ropes round the tree trunk and Tiggy and Daisy helped him to drag it through the garden towards the house.

"A perfect Christmas tree," said Daisy happily.

Tiggy shook her head. "It's not a Christmas tree yet," she said.

"Tiggy's right," Dad said. "It's not a Christmas tree until we've decorated it, is it?"

Decorating the tree was Daisy's favourite thing about Christmas Eve. The very best bit was when Mum turned off all the lamps and Dad turned on the tree lights, transforming the room with special Christmas colours.

As they brought the tree into the kitchen, Mum snatched up something from the table and put it behind her back. Daisy only glimpsed it for a moment. It was brown and thin, with a buckle on the end.

"What's that, Mum?" she asked.

Mum's cheeks turned pink. "Oh, it's nothing," she said. "Just a necklace. Look, Daisy! It's stopped snowing finally. You and Tiggy could build a snowman."

"I'd rather play an imagination game," said Daisy. "Tiggy and I can be explorers."

She looked back out at the garden. It was looking more like the North Pole than ever. The bushes had become fluffy white polar bears and the raised flowerbeds were sleeping seals. The grass was an icy river and Dad's shed was an explorer's hut. And there! Daisy spotted a shape that was no longer a garden bench – it was a sled. Except a sled needed a dog to pull it, and Daisy didn't have a dog.

The perfect dog for pulling the sled would be soft and fluffy with a shaggy head, Daisy decided. It would have a long plumy tail and pricked-up ears, and her fingers would sink deep into its thick fur every time she cuddled it.

She looked again at the whitening garden. Maybe she didn't want to play explorers after all. An idea began fizzing inside her.

"I'm going to build a snowdog," she said.

"Can I help, Daisy?" asked Tiggy.

Daisy looked at her little sister. Tiggy's

idea of helping probably wasn't going to be very helpful at all. Then again, with two of them, they could build the snowdog twice as fast.

"Yes," Daisy decided. "As long as you do what I say."

Tiggy beamed. "I promise."

Back in the garden, Daisy wasted no time in rolling up a big ball of snow in front of the bench.

"Is that the snowdog's head?" Tiggy asked.

Daisy shook her head. "He needs a body first. A fat fluffy body."

Tiggy helped Daisy to roll another ball of snow. They put them together, side by side in front of the bench, and patted snow into the gaps so that it looked like the broad back of a dog lying down on the ground.

"He's a very big dog," said Tiggy. "Is he scary?"

Daisy stroked the snowdog's body. "Of course not," she said. "He's the loveliest, friendliest dog you've ever seen." She added extra snow to give the snowdog paws. "With super-fast legs," she added, "so that when he's pulling our sled, he can run away from polar bears."

Tiggy's eyes grew round. "Polar bears?"

"Don't worry," said Daisy. "He can run

so fast that the polar bears would never catch us."

Tiggy and Daisy rolled another ball of snow to make the dog's head and lifted it on to the body.

"What's his name?" Tiggy wanted to know.

Daisy had known what to call her snowdog the minute she'd thought of making him. It was obvious. "Snowy, of course!" she said with a laugh. "It's the perfect name."

"Will Snowy bark at the polar bears?" Tiggy asked as they shaped the snow and packed it down.

"Definitely," said Daisy, picturing Snowy's booming bark.

Next they scuffed around in the snow,

looking for pebbles. They were hard to find underneath all the soft wet whiteness, but Daisy found two brown ones that were almost the same size for Snowy's eyes, and Tiggy found a shiny black pebble for his nose, and they added a long fat snow tail curled round beside him. The pricked-up ears were trickier – no matter how hard they tried, they couldn't make his ears stick up.

"Maybe his ears have flopped," Tiggy suggested.

Daisy's friend Louise had a dog called Rupert whose ears were always flopping. Yes, Daisy thought. Snowy could have floppy ears. They would be soft and warm, and Snowy would squirm when she tickled them.

When they had finished Snowy's ears, Daisy ran inside to find some reins to help

Snowy pull their sled. She tied four scarves together and looped them over his head. She gave Tiggy one end of the scarf reins and kept the other end for herself.

Tiggy's eyes sparkled with excitement as Daisy swept the snow off the garden-bench sled and helped her to climb on.

"Where are we going?" she breathed.

Daisy grinned. "To find Father Christmas, of course," she said. "Gee up, Snowy!"

Daisy imagined that Snowy began to run. As fast as the wind, faster than the polar bears behind them, Snowy ran on his four big snowy legs towards the sparkling lights of Father Christmas's house. Daisy steered one way and Tiggy steered the other, and they shouted and called instructions as they raced through the wintry landscape.

"Tea!" Mum called.

"That was a good game," said Tiggy as they climbed down from the garden bench.

"It was a brilliant game," said Daisy. She stroked Snowy's floppy ears, imagining his soft, warm, thick fur through her gloves. "Let's play it again tomorrow."

Mum and Dad were sitting in the kitchen when they went back inside. Daisy and Tiggy stamped their feet to shake off the

snow. Now they were inside, Daisy realized that she was actually quite tired. She pulled at her wellies so hard she lost her balance and tumbled sideways against a cupboard. The door opened and four tins rolled out on to the floor. Dad scooped them up quickly and tucked them back on the shelf.

"Why do those tins have dogs on them?" Daisy asked curiously. "What's inside?"

"Oh, it's nothing," said Dad. "Just a new kind of dog spaghetti. Spaghetti in the shape of dogs. A bit like those alphabet ones."

"Yummy!" Tiggy said. "I want dog spaghetti for tea!"

Dad scratched his ear. "Sorry, Tiggy. Your mum's made a shepherd's pie," he said. "Wash your hands now, and we can all have tea."

Daisy washed her hands thoughtfully. Dog spaghetti sounded interesting. She hoped they'd have it soon.

After tea, Daisy and Tiggy helped decorate the tree and arrange the presents underneath. A log crackled in the grate and Daisy and Tiggy's stockings were hung on the mantelpiece. Mum put out a carrot for the reindeer, and Dad placed a mince pie on a plate for Father Christmas.

"This present squeaks," said Tiggy, pressing a red parcel under the tree.

"Maybe it's a mouse," said Mum, glancing at Dad.

"Why would you wrap up a mouse?" asked Daisy.

"As a present for a cat, of course," said Dad.

"But we don't have a cat," said Daisy, feeling puzzled.

Dad clapped his hands. "Come on, girls, bedtime," he said briskly. "The sooner you go to sleep, the sooner Father Christmas will come."

Daisy felt a Christmas thrill deep in her tummy. She took Tiggy's hand and they went up the stairs. As they passed the landing window, Daisy peeped out into the garden. Snowy still lay there beside the garden-bench sled.

"Stay, Snowy," Daisy whispered. "Be a good boy."

Once Daisy was tucked up in bed, she thought about Snowy and all the adventures they could have in the morning. As she drifted off to sleep, she heard raindrops clattering against the window. At one point she thought she heard barking, but she couldn't be sure.

"Christmas!" Tiggy shrieked, jumping on Daisy's bed. "Christmas, Christmas!"

Daisy opened her eyes. The light was greyer than yesterday. Her heart sank to see green leaves and grass from her window where the night before, everything had been white.

"I want to play with Snowy," said Tiggy.

Daisy bit her lip as Tiggy dragged her out of bed. What if the rain had washed Snowy away? They wouldn't have a dog any more.

Daisy risked a glance through the landing

window as Tiggy followed her downstairs. Patches of snow still lay on the ground by the garden bench. She couldn't see Snowy.

Daisy pulled Tiggy past the two fat stockings by the fire, crammed with crinkly packages. She ignored the carrot they had left for the reindeer, which lay half-eaten by the fireplace, and the mince pie just a mess of crumbs on the plate.

"Aren't you going to open your stockings, girls?" Mum called as they ran to the back door.

"In a minute, Mum," Daisy shouted back.

Hopping and swaying, she pulled on her wellies and grabbed Tiggy's hand. Together they went outside into the sparkling morning light.

"Bright," said Tiggy, squinting.

Daisy felt her eyes fill with tears. The bushes weren't polar bears any more, the flowerbeds weren't seals and Dad's shed was just a shed. Beside the garden bench, four scarfs lay tied together on a shapeless mess of snow.

"Where's Snowy gone?" asked Tiggy, looking around.

"He melted," Daisy whispered.

"Dogs don't melt," Tiggy said. She pointed and smiled. "He went that way, see?"

Daisy looked where Tiggy was pointing. Sure enough, there were pawprints in the patches of snow. Daisy stared. Real dog prints!

"Snowy's alive!" Tiggy cried, clapping her hands.

"That's impossible," said Daisy.

"It's not impossible, Daisy," Tiggy insisted. "It's Christmas and magical things happen at Christmas."

Daisy felt her heart swell inside her chest. For a marvellous, magical moment, anything seemed possible. Anything at all.

"Come inside, girls," Mum called from the back door.

Looking behind her at the pawprints, Daisy followed Tiggy into the house.

"Look, Daisy!" said Tiggy.

Sitting in the kitchen was a fluffy white dog with big brown eyes and soft floppy ears, wearing a brown leather collar with a shiny buckle. There was a blue ribbon on his collar and a glittery label with writing on it.

HAPPY CHRISTMAS, DAISY, it said.

Falling to her knees, Daisy stared at the little dog. He got to his feet, wagging his tail, and came towards her.

"It is really you?" she breathed.

She reached for Snowy's ears. She was half expecting them to feel like snow, but they were just as warm as she'd imagined. Snowy rolled on to his back, squirming, and pedalled his legs.

"His eyes are like hot chocolate," said Daisy, laughing. "They're much prettier than the pebbles we used yesterday. Come and stroke him, Tiggy."

Tiggy reached for Snowy and giggled when he licked her fingers.

"There's a present under the tree for him," said Mum.

"Is it the squeaky one?" Daisy guessed.

Tiggy ran to fetch the red present.

"Do you want to give him some food, Daisy?" Dad asked, holding out a familiar tin.

"It isn't dog spaghetti at all!" said Daisy.

Dad grinned and shook his head. Snowy gave a sharp bark.

Daisy laughed, and sank her fingers into Snowy's warm fur. "The polar bears don't stand a chance!" she said.

She had a real dog at last.